PIPER REED

GETS A JOB

W9-AJU-794

KIMBERLY WILLIS HOLT

PiPER REED

GETS A JOB

Illustrated by
CHRISTINE DAVENIER

SQUARE
FISH

HENRY HOLT AND COMPANY
NEW YORK

SQUARE FISH

An Imprint of Macmillan

PIPER REED GETS A JOB. Text copyright © 2009 by Kimberly Willis Holt.
Illustrations copyright © 2009 by Christine Davenier. All rights reserved. Distributed in
Canada by H.B. Fenn and Company Ltd. Printed in May 2010 in the United States of America by
R. R. Donnelley & Sons Company, Harrisonburg, Virginia. For information,
address Square Fish, 175 Fifth Avenue, New York, NY 10010.

Square Fish and the Square Fish logo are trademarks of Macmillan and are used by
Henry Holt and Company under license from Macmillan.

Library of Congress Cataloging-in-Publication Data
Holt, Kimberly Willis.
Piper Reed gets a job / Kimberly Willis Holt ; illustrated by Christine Davenier.
p.   cm.
Summary: When she discovers the price of the coveted clubhouse,
ten-year-old Piper and her fellow Gypsy Club members try
to earn the money by creating a birthday party planning buiness.
ISBN: 978-0-312-60881-1
[1. Business enterprises—Fiction. 2. Parties—Fiction. 3. Birthdays—Fiction.
4. Family life—Florida—Fiction. 5. United States. Navy—Fiction.
6. Pensacola (Fla.)—Fiction.] I. Davenier, Christine, ill. II. Title.
PZ7.H74023Pih 2009   [Fic]—dc22   2008050267

Originally published in the United States by Christy Ottaviano Books,
an imprint of Henry Holt and Company
Square Fish logo designed by Filomena Tuosto
First Square Fish Edition: 2010
10   9   8   7   6   5   4   3   2   1
www.squarefishbooks.com

For my sisters,
Alicia and Angela, with love

—K. W. H.

CONTENTS

PIPER REED
GETS A JOB

1

FiRST Day OF SChOOL

Beep, beep. Six thirty. I turned off the alarm, threw off my covers, and popped out of bed. My insides did flip-flops. There was something exciting about the first day of school. Especially when it was everybody's first day of school. Not like last year, when we moved to Pensacola in October and I was the only new kid in class. This year, the first day of school meant new

notebooks, new pencils, new shoes, new teacher, and a new seat at the back of the class. Everything would be new except for me.

I wondered if Mr. Clark would be my teacher this year. He gave out treat coupons when students got the correct answers. Or maybe I'd be assigned to Mrs. Lindsey. She designed the butterfly garden outside the fifth-grade wing. Her students got extra time outside to take care of the garden.

Instead of sitting in the front of the class like my teacher, Ms. Gordon, made me do last year, I planned to pick a seat at the back near the window. That way I could watch butterflies dart around the salvia in the garden. It was going to be a get-off-the-bus kind of year.

Then I walked inside the school and everything changed. The school secretary grinned at me from behind the registration table.

"Good morning, Piper Reed! How was your summer?"

"How did you know my name?" I asked her. There were hundreds of kids at our school.

"Piper Reed, everyone knows your name. You're famous at Blue Angels Elementary School." She handed me a piece of paper. "Here's your room assignment."

Room 308.

"There must be a mistake—308 was my room last year," I said.

She shook her head. "There's no mistake. We have more fifth-graders this year, so we had to put one class in the fourth-grade hall."

Getting room 308, again, meant I'd have to change my plans. I wouldn't be able to see the butterfly garden. Then I remembered the tree outside the window. Instead of watching butterflies, I'd watch squirrels and birds.

On the way to class, I ran into Michael
and Nicole. Michael didn't look happy either.
"Room 308 again. Boring!"

"I'm in room 405," said Nicole as she headed
toward the *real* fifth-grade hall.

Michael and I walked into 308 together. It
even smelled the same—old paste mixed with
stinky sneakers. We rushed to the back of the
room and chose seats in the row nearest the

* 4 *

window. Outside, a cardinal landed on a branch of the huge tree. Watching birds wasn't like watching butterflies, but it was better than the blackboard.

A moment later, Ms. Gordon walked in. How could a teacher forget it was the first day of school? Maybe she forgot something in her old desk drawer.

"Sorry, Michael and Piper," she said, "but that's not going to work. You two need to take your former seats, where I can keep an eye on you."

I stayed seated. "Ms. Gordon, this is a *fifth*-grade class now."

Just then, Hailey entered the classroom, followed by show-off-know-it-all Kami.

"Hi, Ms. Gordon," Kami said, prancing to the same seat where she sat last year. "I'm so glad you're our teacher again."

I picked up my new notebooks and new

pencil case and walked to my old desk. The first day of school loses all its specialness when you get last year's teacher and have to sit in your same old seat in the same old classroom.

That first week dragged like an ant climbing Mount Everest. We reviewed fractions, learned how to write in different tenses, and studied our vocabulary lists. It was exactly like last year, only Nicole wasn't there. Lucky Nicole got Mrs. Lindsey and had already started working in the butterfly garden.

"We planted purple coneflowers today," she told me. "They attract the Viceroy butterfly."

Finally Saturday arrived. The Gypsy Club was due at my house any minute. Paint fumes filled the living room. Mom was busy painting the backdrop for my big sister, Tori's, middle school play. Her drama coach asked Mom to create it since she was the art teacher at the elementary school. She'd set up a makeshift table out of plywood and two sawhorses. It ran the entire length of the living room, leaving no space for the Gypsy Club. We'd have to find a new place to meet.

Last year, when I was in fourth grade, Mom substituted for our art teacher who was on maternity leave. Now Mrs. Kimmel wanted to stay home with her baby. So Mom got to be the art teacher officially. At first I thought it would be cool having Mom as a teacher, but I soon learned there weren't any benefits. She never said my art projects were the best, even if they were.

My little sister, Sam, was probably the only one who got special treatment because she was six and the baby of the family. My parents thought everything Sam did was spectacular. They practically broke into applause whenever she remembered to feed her goldfish, Peaches the Second.

While I tried to figure out where to hold the meeting, the doorbell rang. I answered the door and found the other three Gypsy Club members—Michael, Nicole, and Hailey.

"Follow me," I told them. We had no choice but to go to my room—the room I shared with Sam. This afternoon, she'd posted a sign on the door that read *QUIET! WRITER AT WORK!*

Inside the room, Sam sat cross-legged on the bed with a thick tablet on her lap. She was probably writing another princess story. That's what spelling bee prodigies do in their spare time. They weren't like normal six-year-old kids who ride bikes and play hide-and-seek. Spelling bee prodigies read and write for fun. Tori wasn't a prodigy, but she liked reading and writing, too. Chief said someone had to break the mold. I guess I was the mold breaker because I hated to read and write.

When we entered the room, Sam frowned. "Hey! I'm busy writing."

Hailey plopped on to Sam's bed.

"I have to have my Gypsy Club meeting here," I told her. "Mom's backdrop is swallowing the living room."

"Well," said Sam, "if you're going to have the meeting here, then I get to be in the Gypsy Club." She was always trying to weasel her way in.

"No way," I told her. "Besides it's my room, too."

Sam glared at Hailey and Nicole. "Then Gypsy Club members aren't allowed on *my* side of the room."

Hailey bounced up from Sam's bed and switched to mine. But Nicole stayed seated. "I love stories," she told Sam. "What is yours about?"

Sam smiled, probably thrilled to have an admirer. "A princess."

"Nicole," I said, "come over on my side. We need to start the meeting."

Nicole slowly inched over the invisible line that now divided our room.

I stood at attention. "Everyone stand so that we can say the Gypsy Club creed."

Together we recited the words that began each meeting. The creed reminded us that we were Navy brats, moving every couple of years or sometimes sooner.

"We are the Gypsies of land and sea. We—"

In a loud voice, Sam said, "Once upon a time . . ."

We ignored her, raising our voices. "We travel from port to port—"

Sam continued, ". . . there lived a beautiful princess in a beautiful castle who had to share a room with her mean, ugly sister."

Nicole stopped and turned toward Sam, but the rest of us kept reciting. "And everywhere we go, we let people know—"

Sam shouted, "Everyone loved the beautiful princess, but no one liked the mean, ugly sister who wouldn't let the beautiful princess be in her club." She stretched out on her stomach.

"Okay," I said, "let's get out of here."

"Great idea!" said Michael.

"Stupendous idea!" said Hailey.

"But I want to hear the rest of Sam's story," said Nicole, looking longingly toward Sam.

Sam stared up from her page. "You can stay."

I grabbed Nicole's hand and led the Gypsy Club out of my room and into Tori's. We'd be safe there since Tori went with her friends to the base movie. At least I thought we'd be safe until the lumpy tower of clothes in the corner started to move toward us.

Hailey gasped.

"What's that?" Nicole yelled.

We froze, waiting for a giant rat to emerge from the pile. Instead our dog, Bruna, popped out from under the blue jeans, T-shirts, and shorts.

"Oh, it's just Bruna," Michael said, but I heard the relief in his voice.

Bruna wagged her tail and went over to each of us, waiting for a pat on the head.

We stepped over the shoes with pointy heels scattered on the floor until we got to a clear spot. Movie star posters covered her wall along with one that said EMILY DICKINSON IS COOL. A framed picture of Ronnie Cartwright was on her nightstand. He didn't give it to Tori. She'd found skateboard boy's image on a Web site and printed it out.

I cleared my throat. "Now as I was trying to say, Halloween is around the corner and—"

"GET OUT OF MY ROOM!" Tori yelled from the doorway. The movie must have ended early. Her face was red.

Her eyes bulged. Her hands curled into fists at her sides.

Nicole took off. She rushed past Tori and down the hall. We heard her feet thump down the steps and the front door squeak open and slam shut.

As Hailey and Michael eased backward out of Tori's room, I tried to explain. "We had no choice."

Tori's hands flew to her hips. "There are always choices. And sneaking into my room is not one of them." She pointed toward the door.

A moment later, Hailey, Michael, and I joined Nicole outside. Nicole wrapped her arms around her body like a ball of tightly wound string. "Your sister is scary."

"Both of my sisters are scary," I said. "They're aliens from Jupiter."

I missed my tree house in San Diego where I could escape Tori and Sam. But after Chief got assigned to NAS Pensacola, Florida, we moved into military housing. Now we lived in a small townhouse with a tiny yard and one puny tree. There was hardly enough room for Bruna to run around.

"We need another meeting place," Hailey muttered. "We could meet at our house, but I have a pesky little brother."

Michael dug in his pocket and pulled out a folded magazine picture. "I have an idea. I was going to show this later, but now is the perfect time."

We watched him slowly unfold the picture until it revealed a clubhouse with a window box and wood shingle roof.

"Get off the bus!" we hollered.

Just then thunder rumbled and a raindrop landed on the tip of my nose. A few seconds later, it began to sprinkle. Then, as if someone flipped a switch, the sprinkle turned into a downpour.

When we dashed inside the townhouse, I accidentally knocked over a can of paint next to the sawhorse. Periwinkle poured out onto the drop cloth, forming a puddle.

"Piper!" Mom yelled.

We needed that clubhouse quick.

2

A Gypsy Dream

When the rain stopped, the Gypsy Club members wiped off their bike seats and rode home. Michael took the picture of the clubhouse with him, but I remembered every detail—the window box in front of the four-pane window, the wood shingle roof, the arched door with a peephole. That peephole would come in handy for keeping out non–Gypsy Club members, mainly Sam.

The magazine ad said the price was *only* 1999

dollars. Nineteen hundred and ninety-nine dollars sounded like a lot of money. But if I said nineteen-ninety-nine it wouldn't sound too expensive. At least I hoped Chief and Mom would think that. I'd find out at dinner when I asked them if they would buy it. The other Gypsy Club members planned to ask their parents, too. One of us was bound to get a yes.

The strong smell of fish sauce drifted through the house. Tonight was Guam night. Every Saturday night Mom picked a place where we'd lived and chose recipes she'd learned to make there. Last week was Corpus Christi, Texas, night. We ate fried shrimp and French fries. The week before was San Diego, California. Mom baked vegetarian lasagna. But tonight she pulled out the big pot to cook *pancet*. One of our neighbors on Guam was from the Philippines. She taught Mom to make the noodle dish with all kinds of vegetables. It tasted pretty good if you ate around the vegetables.

Mom also fried *lumpia*, which reminded me of giant spring rolls. I loved dipping them in the tangy sweet-and-sour sauce, then biting into the crispy layers.

Sam acted like she invented Guam night since she was born on the island. She began every sentence at dinner that night by saying, "Since I was born on Guam. . . ."

Toward the end of the meal, she stabbed a carrot and asked, "Since I was born on Guam, did I get to swim with the tropical fish?"

"You were too little," Mom said.

"But I did." I remembered snorkeling with Chief and Tori in the ocean. We had to wear our tennis shoes so that the coral didn't cut our feet. Under the water, we discovered turkey fish, angel fish, and butterfly fish. I was about six years old. Since I hadn't learned to swim very well, I wore a safety vest, and Chief stood over me, making sure I didn't swallow too much water.

"I remember the sea slugs," Tori said. "Yuk!"

"And climbing a coconut tree in our front yard," I added.

Tori made a snapping sound with her tongue. "You did not climb our coconut tree."

I shrugged. "Well, I tried."

"That doesn't count," said Tori. "Loan's brother climbed the coconut tree."

Loan was our Vietnamese neighbor who had married a Navy chief. Her brother climbed to the top of the coconut tree and cut the green coconuts with a machete. I didn't like green coconuts because of their slimy texture.

Suddenly Sam blurted, "Since I was born on Guam, would you buy me a tropical fish aquarium?"

Talk about rotten timing. Just when I'd planned to hit Mom and Dad up for some money, Sam beat me to it. That tropical fish aquarium would make it harder for me to get the clubhouse.

"Well . . ." Mom started.

"Why don't you buy it yourself?" I asked. "You're rich. You have all that money in your piggy bank."

Sam lowered her eyebrows and frowned. "I don't have enough for a tropical fish aquarium."

That aquarium must have cost too much if Sam didn't have enough. She'd saved every penny she'd ever gotten.

"Speaking of money," Tori began, "the poetry club is taking a trip to England for spring break. I'd really like to go."

"Gosh, Tori, I don't know," Chief said. "How much does that cost?"

"Two thousand dollars," Tori mumbled.

Mom's eyes widened. "Two thousand dollars? That's a lot of money."

Tori leaned in, her hands flying as she spoke. "That includes everything—airfare, hotel, food, and tours for an entire week. England is a must-see for a poet. It's the literary capital of the world. For goodness' sake, don't you want me to visit the home and grave of William Shakespeare?"

Two thousand dollars *was* a lot. My clubhouse was only 1999, and I'd still have it after a week. Not like some trip where all Tori would have was a bunch of pictures when it was over. Maybe I should have waited until dessert, but I decided to jump in, before Tori and Sam wiped out all the money in Mom and Chief's savings account.

I straightened. "Mom, Chief, do I have a bargain for you."

Chief chuckled. "Does it cost two thousand dollars?"

"Heck no," I said.

"That's a relief," he said.

"The clubhouse only costs nineteen-ninety-nine."

Mom's right eyebrow shot up. "Nineteen dollars and ninety-nine cents for a clubhouse?"

"That is a bargain," Chief said. "You know what they say about things that sound too good to be true. They usually are." He took a big swallow of tea.

I gulped. "I meant nineteen hundred and ninety-nine dollars."

The tea sprayed from Chief's mouth. He wiped his face with his napkin and said, "Girls, we aren't rich like the Trumps from New York.

I'm a Navy chief and your mom is a teacher. If you really want those things, you'll have to figure out a way to make extra income."

"What if we do more chores?" Tori asked.

"I could mow the lawn," I said. I'd always wanted to push the mower around the yard. It would be kind of like driving a car.

Mom shook her head. "Girls, we can't afford to pay more allowance than you already receive.

You'll have to figure out another way. Tori, maybe you could babysit."

Tori folded her arms across her chest. "I'd have to babysit a year to make two thousand dollars."

"What can I do?" Sam asked.

I was thinking the same question.

"Put your thinking cap on," Mom said. "Be creative."

I decided before I did that I'd call the other Gypsy Club members and find out what answer they got from their parents. I just wished one of their last names was Trump.

3

PLAN B

I called Michael and Nicole first.

Michael answered the phone. "Well?" I said. "What did your parents say?"

"No, no, and no with a cherry on top."

"Huh?"

Michael explained, "I asked them. They said, 'No.' I said, 'Please!'" They said, 'No.' Then I said, 'Please with a cherry on top.' They said, 'No with a cherry on top!'"

"Well, maybe Hailey's parents said yes."

"Hold on," Michael said. "Nicole wants to speak to you."

The phone was silent for a moment, then I heard Nicole's voice. "Hi, Piper."

"Hi, Nicole."

"Is Sam there?"

"Sam? Why do you want to talk to Sam?"

"I wanted to hear the rest of her princess story."

"Her sign is on the door." This time Sam had added DO NOT DISTURB above WRITER AT WORK.

"Well, tell her hello from me."

"Okay."

"And tell her I can't wait to hear the rest of the story."

"Sure." It was hard to believe Nicole and Michael were related, much less twins.

Next I called Hailey. She didn't even wait for me to ask.

"My parents said, 'No way. Money doesn't grow on trees.'"

"I guess that means you'll have to get a job just like me."

"A job? I'm ten years old. What kind of job can I get?"

"I don't know, but I'm sure you'll think of something. Your part will be five hundred dollars."

"Piper, it just might as well be five million dollars."

"Where's that Gypsy spirit?" I asked before hanging up and calling Michael and Nicole again.

"Hailey's parents said no, too. Looks like you and Nicole will each have to earn five hundred dollars. That gives us one penny left over for tax."

Michael cleared his throat. "Piper, I hate to

tell you this, but sales tax will be a lot more than a penny. It's the little details that can do you in."

Michael always did like to show off about being good at math.

"Well," I told him, "we can worry about that later."

I walked outside with Bruna, trying to think of a way to earn money. My next-door neighbors, Brady and his mom, Yolanda, were out in the yard. Brady dropped his bucket and waved from his sandbox. "Hi, Boona! Hi, Piper!"

"Hi, Brady!"

"I'm almost twee!"

"Yes, I know." Brady had claimed he was three since they moved in ten months ago. Yolanda always corrected him, adding, "Almost." Then I realized he probably *was* almost three. So I asked, "When is your birthday?"

"September 15."

Today was the first of the month. Brady was finally officially almost three years old.

"That's really great, Brady! Happy almost-birthday."

I went inside the house and grabbed a snicker-doodle cookie from the cookie jar. Before my first bite, I gave the cookie a long sniff, inhaling the cinnamon scent. I couldn't remember my third birthday, but I do remember my fourth. It was the first birthday party I had with friends. Chief blew up lots of balloons, and Mom made a circus birthday cake. There were loads of games and presents.

Get off the bus! Just thinking about that birthday party made my mind explode. I had a spectacular idea for a job. I went to Mom's art trunk and pulled out a piece of heavy cardboard and some red paint. Then, even though I was so excited I could hardly stand it, I took a big breath and painted the words as neatly as possible.

Piper Reed
Birthday Party Planner
Most Fun for the Best Prices
Guaranteed

It was dusk when I finished the words. Then I went outside to hammer the sign into the ground. I picked a great spot, right smack in the middle of our front yard, facing the street.

Yolanda and Brady had already gone inside. That's okay, I thought. Maybe Brady's dad, Abe, would see the sign when he arrived home. Then they'd call and I'd have a job. My first job of many because I'd earn a great reputation as a birthday party planner. Every mom and dad on the base would want to hire me. I could almost touch that Gypsy clubhouse.

At dinner, Mom called for Sam to come to the table. She even had to resort to yelling, "Samantha Reed, get to the dinner table this instant."

We were all seated, ready to eat, except for Sam. Finally we heard the bedroom door swing open and hit the wall. Next we heard her slowly moving down the stairs—*shlump, shlump, shlump*.

She shuffled into the kitchen, her crown fixed on her head and a pencil tucked behind her ear.

After she slipped into her chair, Sam announced, "I have a job."

Chief grinned. "Oh?"

"I'm an author."

"Don't you have to be published to be an author?" I asked.

"I will be," she said, and the way Sam said it, I believed her.

Mom smiled and passed the mashed potatoes. "An author? How glamorous!"

Sam frowned. "There is nothing glamorous about being an author. It's hard work. My fingers hurt from writing, and my head hurts from trying to think of story ideas."

"What's with the crown?" I asked. "I thought you put that away forever."

"Authors have to have inspiration. My crown is the inspiration for my princess stories."

"Well, that's nothing special," I said. "I'm a birthday party planner."

Tori groaned. "Great! Both my little sisters have jobs, but not me."

Mom gasped. "Oh, Tori. I almost forgot. Yolanda said Mrs. Milton was looking for a babysitter on Saturdays while she works at her interior decorating business."

Tori's eyes bulged. "The Milton Monsters! No thanks. Everyone knows those six-year-old triplets are triple trouble."

Mom shrugged. "She's paying double."

"Hey," I said, "Shouldn't she pay triple if they're triplets?"

"Double?" Tori twisted her mouth. I could tell she was chewing on the idea. Making some money could help her get to England.

"Just remember," I said, "home and grave of William Shakespeare."

"I'll sleep on the idea," Tori said before taking a big spoonful of peas.

"You might not want to wait," Mom said. "Yolanda said Mrs. Milton posted the job on the commissary bulletin board. Someone else might have already beat you to it."

After dinner, Tori decided she would call Mrs. Milton about the job.

"Don't stay on the phone too long," I told Tori. "I am expecting a very important business call."

Tori left a message for Mrs. Milton. Thirty minutes later she returned her call. Tori had a job.

The phone didn't ring again the remainder of the night. Before school the next morning I turned the sign so that it faced Brady's house. Yolanda and Abe were sure to notice my sign now. But when I arrived home there was only one phone message and it was from Chief. He told Mom not to cook dinner. We'd go out for hamburgers.

Maybe Abe and Yolanda couldn't see my sign. I moved it onto the border between our yards. How could they miss it now? But the phone still hadn't rung by the time Chief got home.

After Chief changed from his uniform into jeans and a white shirt, we went off-base to McDonald's. "Our three girls have jobs. Now that's something to celebrate!"

Tori glanced up from her French fries. "Well, I'm really the only one with a *real* job."

"I have a real job!" Sam said. "I'm an author."

Tori rolled her eyes. "You haven't sold a book yet."

I turned to Sam. "I'll buy one!"

"See," Sam said, "I'm an author. I haven't even finished my story and I've already sold a copy."

Tori let out a long dramatic sigh. Then she glared at me. "But you haven't booked a birthday party."

"She can plan *my* birthday party," Sam said.

"Thank you, Sam," I said.

"You're welcome very much." Sam took a bite of her Chicken McNugget.

"Like I said, all three of our daughters have jobs." He lifted his paper cup and said, "Here's to the Reed girls. Each of them industrious."

We all raised our sodas and clinked them together. I could tell Tori didn't want to. She liked thinking she was the only one with a real job. I hated to admit it, but she was right. Sam's birthday didn't come until November. It was still September.

When we returned home, Tori went to her room to do her homework. Sam took off to our room to write her book. I peeked between the drapes to check on the sign.

It was gone! Someone had stolen my sign. Probably a competitor.

Just then, the doorbell rang.

"Piper!" Chief called me to the door. "Abe wants to speak to you."

Abe stood in the doorway, holding my sign in his hand. "Piper, I think someone accidentally moved your sign into our yard."

"Oh?" I tried to act surprised.

Chief raised his eyebrows. "Did you post this sign in Abe's yard?"

"Yes sir. I wanted to get the word out."

Chief shook his head. "Piper, it's not very neighborly to make holes in someone's yard."

My face burned. "I'm sorry."

Abe smiled so big, his dimples showed. "Don't worry about the holes. I just didn't want you to lose your sign." He handed it back to me.

Then he asked, "Are you serious about this birthday party planning?"

"Yes sir."

"Super! Yolanda and I would like to hire you to help with Brady's birthday party. The big day is thirteen days away. Does that give you enough time?"

"I can plan a party in thirteen days."

"I have to warn you, Brady is very picky about what he wants. In fact, he's kind of exhausting. Are you up to the challenge?"

"Piper Reed Birthday Party Planners offers the most fun with the best prices."

"Could you meet with Yolanda and Brady tomorrow morning at nine?"

I saluted. "Affirmative. Piper Reed at your service."

Abe shook Chief's hand *and* mine before saying good-bye.

When the door closed, Chief wrapped his arm around my shoulders. "Looks like my three girls have real jobs after all. Congratulations, Piper."

4

PiPER REED, BiRThDAY PARTY PLANNER

Saturday morning Tori left for her babysitting job and I went over to Brady's house. I brought a notebook to write down important ideas.

Abe wasn't there because he worked Saturdays. So Yolanda and I settled at the kitchen table. Brady sat between us, propped on his booster chair.

"How about some doughnuts and chocolate milk?" Yolanda asked.

"Thank you," I said. My job had great perks!

After pouring two cups of chocolate milk, Yolanda set a plate of pink frosted doughnuts with sprinkles in front of me. "Tell Piper what kind of birthday party you'd like, Brady."

"I want a birdday cake."

"Yes, of course." I opened my notebook and drew a birthday cake with three candles. This was going to be easy.

Brady shook his head. "No!"

"No birthday cake?"

"I want an aztoonot birdday cake."

"An astronaut?"

Brady nodded.

I drew an astronaut on top of a cake. He looked pretty cool with his helmet and moon-walking boots.

Brady shook his head. "No!"

Yolanda picked up my drawing and examined it. "Brady, this *is* an astronaut. A very good astronaut, I might add."

"Thank you," I said.

Brady shook his head. "No, I want twee aztoonots."

"I get it," I said. "You're going to be three years old. So you want an astronaut for each year."

"Yep," Brady said.

I drew three astronauts while Brady leaned toward me, watching.

"Yep," Brady said as I finished. "Twee aztoonots."

"Okay. How about entertainment? Do you want a magician or a clown? Or maybe you'd like some fun games?"

I didn't know any magicians or clowns, but I'd find one. After all, Brady's birthday was thirteen days away.

"Yep." Brady nodded, tapping the table like a Congo drum.

"Which one? A magician?"

"Yep, and all the other stuff."

"Magician, clowns, *and* games?"

"Yep! Yep!" Brady clapped his hands.

"Brady," Yolanda said, "Piper cannot do all of that."

"Sure I can," I said. "Piper Reed Birthday Party Planners promise to be the best birthday planning service."

Yolanda's eyebrows touched. "Are you sure you can do all that? A magician and a clown could cost a lot."

"We promise the best prices. I better get started." I knew exactly who to hire. I grabbed a doughnut before heading home. Owning a business had responsibilities. I had lots of work to do.

At home I called the Gypsy Club members and told them to meet at my house Monday after school. Now they would have jobs, too.

Meanwhile I thought of some games Brady might like to play—Pin the Astronaut on the Moon, Musical Spaceship Chairs, Find the Alien.

Right before dinner, Tori walked into the house after babysitting. A spooky witch version of Tori. Patches of her hair frizzed out like she'd stuck a finger in an electrical socket. A big green spot covered the front of her blouse. "Those Milton triplets are monsters. I'm quitting!"

"You can't quit," Mom said. "Mrs. Milton is counting on you, Tori."

"Well, she can count on someone else."

Mom sighed. "It's only until she gets that big

job finished. Then you can quit. But you made a commitment, young lady. And you are going to stick to it. Reeds honor their commitments."

"Then I'm changing my last name." Tori stomped off to her bedroom, slamming the door behind her.

Mom didn't need to worry about me quitting. Piper Reed Birthday Party Planners always honored our commitments.

After school Monday, I waited for the Gypsy Club to show up. Meanwhile Sam twirled into the living room and plopped down on the sofa. "I finished writing my first Princess Samantha book. Now I have to illustrate it."

"What's your story called?" I asked.

"*Princess Samantha, Ruler of the Fair Land of NAS Pensacola.*"

"No one will remember your title," I told her. "It's too long."

"No it's not."

"Well, even if it's not, princesses don't rule military bases. Navy officers do."

Sam glared at me. "This is a fairy tale. Anything can happen in a fairy tale."

I sighed.

Tori walked through with Chief's old football helmet.

"Are you trying out for the football team?" I asked.

She smirked. "Of course not. This is for protection."

"From what?"

"Protection from those Milton Monsters. I don't want a head injury. The next time they tackle me, I'll be prepared."

"I thought you were going to quit."

She scowled. "And blemish the Reed name?"

The Miltons lived a few streets over, but Tori was running late, so Mom drove her to their house.

A few minutes later, the Gypsy Club arrived.

"What's this meeting about?" Hailey asked. "We need to hurry because I have a lot of homework."

"Yeah, this better be good," Michael said. "I'm missing my favorite show."

"I have jobs for all of you," I told them.

"Why do we need jobs?" Hailey asked.

"Remember the clubhouse?" How could they have forgotten already?

"We're never going to get that clubhouse," Hailey said. "It costs too much."

"Yeah," Michael said. "You're just dreaming."

"I am a dreamer," I said. "Dreams are where all good ideas start." Mom said that a lot. "I've started a birthday party planning business. My next-door neighbors, Yolanda and Abe, hired me to plan their son's birthday party. And now I need some assistants."

"I want a job," Nicole said.

I grabbed my notebook. "First you have to interview for them."

"What kind of jobs?" Michael asked.

"There are three jobs—a clown, a magician, and a baker."

"Why can't we just pick a job?" Hailey asked.

"That's not the way Piper Reed Birthday Party Planners work. We're professionals."

A big grin spread across Nicole's face, showing a good view of the red, white, and blue rubber bands on her braces. "I want to be the clown."

"You aren't even funny," Michael said. "Clowns are funny."

Nicole lifted her chin. "Then why are you always laughing at me?"

"Because you're a goofball," Michael said.

"That's great," I said. "Clowns should be goofy. You've got a job!" I held my hand out to Nicole.

She shook my hand as she grinned, flashing her shiny braces. "That was easy!"

Hailey bounced in place. "I want to be the magician."

Michael's eyes bulged. "Hey, I'm the guy. I should be the magician."

"Who said a magician had to be a guy?" I asked.

"Yeah," Hailey said. "Your mother is a Navy officer. What if someone said she couldn't do that because she's a woman?"

Michael turned red.

"That's right," I said. "Being a guy doesn't make you more magical. You have to meet the qualifications."

"What are the qualifications?" he asked.

I looked down at my notebook. "Can you do any magic tricks?"

Michael didn't say anything.

Then Hailey spoke. "I can do a card trick."

I dug in the junk drawer of the desk and found Chief's poker cards. I handed them to Hailey.

Hailey shuffled the cards. Then, without looking at them, she dealt ten cards and fanned them out so that I could see only the face side. "Pick one."

I chose the Queen of Hearts. Then I gave it back to her facedown.

Hailey tucked the card back into the deck with the others and shuffled them again. She went through each card, turning them over. "Nope, nope, nope . . . ," she muttered.

When the Queen of Hearts appeared, Hailey

stopped and held it up, showing each of us. "This is the one you picked."

"How'd you do that?" Nicole asked.

"Magic," Hailey said. Then she stuck out her tongue at Michael.

"You've got a job," I told her, sealing the deal with a shake.

"What does that leave me?" Michael asked.

I handed him the picture I'd drawn of Brady's astronaut cake.

Michael scrunched up his face and scratched his head. "Huh?"

"*Bon appétit*, Chef Michael," I said.

"I don't know how to bake a cake."

I shrugged. "Can't you find a recipe in a cookbook?"

"Well . . ." Michael studied the picture. "How am I going to make those astronauts?"

"Don't worry. I can draw and paint them on cardboard. Then you can stick them on the cake."

A few minutes later they left, and I went to my room. Sam was sitting on the bed, her legs crossed at the ankles as she colored. She frowned and dropped a pink crayon.

"What's wrong?" I asked. "Did the princess run into the admiral?"

Sam threw the crayon across the room. It hit the wall before falling to the floor. "I write better than I draw. No one will want to buy my book if the pictures aren't good."

She kicked the wall so hard that Mom heard and ordered her outside to run laps around the yard with Bruna. "Burn off some of that steam, Samantha Reed."

When she stomped from the room, I picked up her drawing pad. Sam was right. Drawing wasn't her thing. But it was mine.

I took a piece of a paper and wrote down the following:

Superb Illustrator for Hire
For more information contact Piper Reed

Then I taped the sign on to the door. A few moments later Sam came back into the room, holding my sign. Sweat beads covered her forehead. Bruna walked in behind her and plopped next to me on the floor. She was still panting from the run.

"How much?" Sam asked. Her right eyebrow raised as she waited.

"Half of the profits," I told her.

"But it's *my* story."

"Take it or leave it."

Sam put her finger to her temple and tapped her foot. She stared at me for a long time, but I wasn't backing down.

She sighed long and hard. "Okay. But you'll have to meet my deadline."

Get off the bus! I could almost see that Gypsy clubhouse in our backyard.

5

DEADLiNES

"Your deadline is September 12," Sam told me.

"That's three days before Brady's birthday party!"

"And two days before my book signing."

"Where are you going to do a book signing?"

Sam rolled her eyes as if she couldn't believe I wouldn't know. "At a bookstore."

I didn't have anything to worry about. No bookstore would allow a six-year-old to sell books, even if she was a prodigy.

The next day at school, Ms. Gordon assigned a huge project. She wrote a whole bunch of famous names on the blackboard. Right away I noticed Amelia Earhart's.

"This month's project is a biographical paper," Ms. Gordon said. "You must select a name on the board. Later this morning, you'll have a chance to write your name next to that person's. Your assignment will be to research and write a report about your subject."

Ms. Gordon asked Kami to hand out the project papers that explained the due dates of each step. Then she continued talking. "I am trusting each of you to do the research and organize your notes on index cards. First drafts are due in a week. Final drafts are due on the seventeenth."

The seventeenth was the Monday following Brady's party. That would give me plenty of time. I read some of the names: Benjamin Franklin, Thomas Jefferson, Harriet Tubman. I didn't bother to read the rest because I planned to choose Amelia Earhart.

Just then Ms. Mitchell, the Special Ed teacher, entered our room to get me for reading. Since I was special because of my dyslexia I got to visit her class every day. Last year I went in the afternoons, but this year my time moved to the morning before lunch.

Thirty minutes later when I returned to my classroom, there were a lot more names on the board. All my classmates. Everyone had chosen a subject except for me. And there next to Amelia Earhart was Kami's name spelled out with her curlicue letters and the heart she used to dot her *i*. The only name left was Cyrus McCormick.

"Who is he?" I asked Michael at recess.

He shrugged. "Heck if I know. I picked Benjamin Franklin. Everyone knows him. And he's interesting."

"Do you know who Cyrus McCormick is?" I asked Hailey. She thought she knew everything.

"I think he invented pepper," she said.

Finally I asked Ms. Gordon.

"That's a good place to start your research,

Piper. Look him up when we go to the library later."

At two o'clock, we went to the library to research our topics. All the kids buzzed over to the biography section. I thumbed through the drawing books until the line thinned out. I didn't have to worry. I was sure the books about Cyrus McCormick would be on the shelf. Who'd want to check them out? But when I searched through the *M* shelf there wasn't one book about him.

I went over to Ms. Gordon. "Are you sure you spelled his name right?"

Ms. Gordon's eye started to twitch. "Yes, Piper Reed. Check your other sources."

I decided to ask Mrs. Keller, the librarian. Surely a librarian was the best library source. Mrs. Keller was round and wore fuzzy sweaters. A magnet on her desk had a picture of a sheep and read, "I'm not fat, just fluffy."

"Mrs. Keller," I said, "my topic is Cyrus McCormick, but I can't find out anything. There are no books about him in our library."

She twisted up her mouth. "Hmm. Cyrus McCormick? I wonder who he is."

I knew I was in trouble when the librarian didn't even know my biographical subject.

"Well," Mrs. Keller said, "it will be like a treasure hunt. That's what's fun about research."

Somehow I didn't think a chest of gold would be at the end of this treasure hunt.

We went to the computer and researched Cyrus McCormick on the Internet. After clicking on a few sites, we discovered Cyrus McCormick was the inventor of the reaper, a machine that cuts grain.

Mrs. Keller only said, "Oh."

"I wanted Amelia Earhart," I told her, "but someone else beat me to it."

Mrs. Keller flicked her wrist. "Everyone knows about Amelia Earhart, but you have the opportunity to tell your class about someone they've probably never heard of."

When she said that it made me think of Mom trying to get me to eat yucky spinach, pretending it was as delicious as an orange Dreamsicle just because it was good for you. Maybe Cyrus McCormick was like spinach. Maybe knowing about him was good for you. I thought about this for a second. I still would have preferred Amelia Earhart.

At dinner, Tori looked happier than she'd been since she started babysitting the Milton triplets. She announced, "I know how I'm going to earn enough money for England and it has nothing to do with babysitting triple trouble."

"How?" I asked.

She pulled out a flyer. "The Scrabble championship at the convention center. Grand prize: five thousand dollars. Saturday, September 15."

"Only one problem," Mom said. "Saturdays you have a babysitting job."

Tori lowered her shoulders. "But, Mom, this is a once-in-a-lifetime chance. Besides, it's over by noon."

"Your mom is right," Chief said. "The only way you can enter is if you find a replacement for your babysitting job that morning."

After dinner, I hurried to my room and took out my drawing pad. I wrote:

Substitute Babysitter
Available for Hire
Morning of September 15
Contact Piper Reed

Then I hung the sign on Tori's door. How bad could babysitting the Milton triplets be? Besides, I was more fun than Tori. And even though it was the same day as Brady's birthday, the party wouldn't start until three o'clock.

Before bedtime, Tori knocked on my door. A moment later, I had another job.

6

JOB PRESSURE

I needed to research Cyrus McCormick, but I also had to illustrate Sam's book. Cyrus would have to wait.

Sam's manuscript started, "Once upon a time . . ." Not a very original beginning. Although I guess a story about a princess who ruled over a military base was an original idea. But Sam used long words, probably to show off. What did "discontented" mean? If I was going to do the pictures I had to find out.

I went to the bookshelf in the hall to find the dictionary. But it wasn't there. The last time I'd used the dictionary was to press flowers for one of Mom's art projects. Maybe it was in Tori's room. Sure enough, the huge book covered the entire nightstand. Post-it Notes stuck to some of the pages. Tori must have been practicing for the Scrabble competition. A tablet with a list of words rested on top of the dictionary. Only instead of long words like Sam put in her story, small words made up Tori's list—*quip, vita, zed, flog.*

I'd never played Scrabble, but surely longer words were better. How did Tori think she would win that competition with those itty-bitty words? I opened the dictionary and searched for "discontented." *Wanting something more or different.* Why didn't Sam just say that if that's what it meant?

For some reason, looking up words in the dictionary made me as hungry as an hour of swimming. I went downstairs for a snack. Just as I was about to take a bite of my peanut butter sandwich, I heard Sam holler, "This is all wrong!"

Soon she appeared in front of me, waving my drawing. "There are no astronauts in my story."

"Those astronauts aren't for your story. They're for Brady's birthday cake."

"Where are *my* sketches?" Sam asked.

"You mean *my* sketches. *I'm* doing the illustrations."

"Well, where are they?"

"I haven't started them yet."

"What do you mean you haven't started them yet?"

"Just what I said."

"What about my book signing?"

"Don't worry. They'll be ready for your book signing."

"They better be."

"What's your hurry? You don't even have a store lined up yet."

Sam raised her chin. "Yes I do."

"Where?"

"Mr. Sanchez's store."

"Mr. Sanchez? He owns a pet store."

"He has books, too."

"Books on raising pets, not princesses who rule Navy bases."

"He said he wanted to expand."

How did I get stuck with two wacky sisters? "I'm going outside for some fresh air."

I took Bruna out back and threw the ball. She still hadn't mastered that trick. But she was better than she used to be. Today she chased after the ball and ran around the yard about twenty times until she got tired. Then she dropped the ball a few inches from my feet.

Brady was playing in his sandbox. When he noticed us, he hollered, "Hi, Boona!"

Bruna ran over to Brady and dropped the ball at his feet. I hated when that happened. It was hard to accept that an almost three-year-old was better at teaching my dog tricks than I was.

"Hey, Piper, I have some more birdday stuff," Brady said.

"You mean birthday gifts?"

"Nope, stuff for my birdday potty."

"Just a second." I picked up Bruna and headed toward Brady's yard.

Brady cupped his hands around his mouth. "Better get your notebook."

"Why?"

"You might forget. And it's very important stuff."

"I have an excellent memory. Trust me."

"I want a spaceship."

"A real spaceship?" I was about to explain to Brady that I didn't know anyone at NASA when he shook his head and giggled.

"No, silly. On my birdday cake, next to the twee aztoonots."

"Oh, okay." I could draw a spaceship.

"And a wabbit."

"A rabbit on the cake? You mean a space rabbit?"

"No. A weal wabbit out of a hat."

"You mean the magician's hat?"

"Yep."

I scratched my temple. "Um. I'll have to see about that."

"You said, 'Piper Reed Birdday Potty Planners is the mostest fun.'"

If there was anything I couldn't stand, it was

to be reminded of my business creed by an almost three-year-old.

"Okay. Of course. One live rabbit. No problem." Maybe Mr. Sanchez would let me borrow a rabbit. If he allowed Sam to do a book signing at his store, surely he could part with one tiny rabbit.

Brady wasn't finished yet. "And I want a clown that jiggles."

"Jiggles?

"Throws balls up and catches them."

"Juggles?"

"Yep."

"How many balls?

Brady scratched his chin and paused a second. "Um . . . fifty-five."

"I don't know about that," I told him. "But I'll try to get the clown to juggle."

"And . . . and . . ."

"I've got to go inside, Brady. Sam needs me

to illustrate her book. I'll see you later. Come on, Bruna."

I needed to escape Brady before he made any more demands. He was worse than Sam. Now I had to schedule an emergency Gypsy Club meeting. Quick!

7

INSPIRATION

"**A** rabbit?" Hailey snapped. "I can't pull a real rabbit out of a hat."

"Why not?" I asked. "Have you ever tried?"

"No. For one thing, I don't have a real rabbit. You need to have a real rabbit before you pull one out of a hat."

"No problem," I said. "I'll find a rabbit for you."

For some reason, that didn't seem to make Hailey happy.

Nicole tossed a wadded piece of paper toward the ceiling and tried to catch it. It dropped to the ground. "I don't know how to juggle," she said, "but I can learn."

"That's the Gypsy spirit!" I told her.

Michael removed the top from a plastic container. A sweet aroma drifted from the box. "How about a cupcake?"

We looked down at four chocolate cupcakes with chocolate frosting. We all took one except for Nicole.

"Don't you want a cupcake?" I asked before taking a bite. Maybe she knew something we didn't. After all, she lived with Michael. Maybe he handled his guinea pig, Tippy-Toes, and didn't wash his hands before touching the chocolate chips. "Is something wrong with them?"

Nicole shook her head. "No, that's not it. Michael's been baking cupcakes every day since he became the baker. I think I might be allergic to them."

My tongue traveled around the edge of the cupcake. "To chocolate?"

"Chocolate cupcakes," Nicole said. "I think I have a chocolate cupcake allergy."

"I've never heard of a chocolate cupcake allergy." I took a big bite.

Michael frowned. "That's because there really isn't one."

"Well, I think they're delicious," I said.

Michael straightened. "I want to find the best recipe for Brady's cake. That takes practice."

"That's why our freezer is filled with cupcakes." Nicole sighed.

"Get off the bus!" I said. "A freezer filled with chocolate cupcakes? I could handle that."

"Michael, I was thinking." Hailey's voice sounded different—sweet and gooey. "If you still want to be the magician, I guess I could bake the birthday cake. Just give me the recipe and the magician job is all yours."

"No way," Michael said. "I do all the hard work and you get all the glory?"

Nicole tossed the wad of paper again. This time she caught it. "Michael likes baking."

Hailey smirked. "You do?"

Michael turned red. "Well, yeah. What's wrong with that?"

"Nothing," Hailey said. "My mom and grandma like to bake, too. They wear floral aprons when they bake. Do you wear a floral apron?"

Michael snapped his tongue against his mouth. "Oh, I get it. You think baking is for girls. Guess what? If a magician can be a girl, a baker can be a boy."

"Well," I said. "It sounds like everyone has their perfect job."

"And what are you doing, Piper?" Hailey asked. "Just how are you helping with the party? It seems like we're doing all the hard work."

"Someone has to be in charge. It's not easy dealing with clients, especially Brady." Of course, I didn't remind them that Brady was our only client.

"Hey, Nicole, if you're not going to eat that cupcake, can I have it?" I didn't wait for her to answer. I just grabbed it. After all I was the president and founder of Piper Reed Birthday Party Planners. I should have some privileges.

Before I ended the meeting, Hailey asked, "How am I supposed to practice pulling a rabbit out of a hat?"

"Just a second." I ran upstairs and dug through the closet for the old stuffed bunny I got one Easter. For a year, I couldn't fall asleep unless I took Mr. Bunny to bed with me, but I was only four then. It wasn't like I was attached to it the way Sam was to her doll, Annie.

Back downstairs, I held out Mr. Bunny to Hailey. "Practice pulling this out of a hat until you have a chance to try it with the real thing." Nicole grabbed Mr. Bunny by a tattered ear. "Hey," I said. "Don't carry him like that. Mr. Bunny doesn't—"

Michael cracked up. "*Mr. Bunny?* Careful, Hailey. Mr. Bunny doesn't like to be held like that."

My face burned, but Hailey didn't seem to hear Michael. "Where am I going to find out *how* to pull a rabbit out of a hat?"

I shrugged. "Don't ask me, Hailey. You're the magician."

She groaned. "Stop reminding me."

As they left, I hollered, "Nicole, don't forget to practice juggling. Michael, keep up the great work."

I went upstairs to my room where Sam was sitting on her bed next to Annie. When she noticed me, she crossed her arms over her chest and made tiny slits with her eyes. She was probably mad because I hadn't started on her illustrations.

A twinge of guilt wriggled inside me. I picked up my drawing pad, but the blank page just stared back. My head felt empty. I scribbled. Nothing. I felt Sam's eyes piercing a hole through me. I glanced up. Just as I suspected. She was watching me, still frowning, still squinting.

"How do you expect me to draw while you're staring at me?"

Sam pretended to yawn, stretching her arms to the ceiling. "I didn't say anything."

"You don't have
to say anything.
I know what
you're thinking."

"Oh, so you
can't draw,
but you can
read minds?"

"Sam, you
are not going to
make me draw. I'll
draw when I'm good
and ready. And I'm not ready."

After putting the pad on my nightstand, I
marched out of the room and nearly tripped
over Bruna, who was waiting on the other side
of our door. She followed me down the hall. She
was always following the person that she
thought might take her for a walk. I grabbed
her leash and we headed outside.

Walking on a leash was something else Bruna hadn't quite figured out how to do yet. She either ran too fast, forcing me to huff and puff to keep up with her, or she plopped and flopped in the middle of the road. When that happened, I had to drag her along. Today turned out to be a huff and puff day, which suited me just fine. I felt like running.

We sprinted down the street toward the park. I wished that I could go all the way to the beach and the lighthouse, but Mom and Chief thought that was too far. Suddenly I imagined Princess Samantha gazing out of a lighthouse window. What if she lived in the base lighthouse?

Bruna and I raced around the park and toward the officers' housing. Maybe the prince lived in one of the officers' houses. When we reached the end of their block, we turned around and ran all the way back. My heart pounded. Ideas started to spin in my head—ideas for illustrations.

By the time I reached home, the sun had sunk low in the sky. Dinner was ready and my entire family sat around the table, staring at me.

"Piper, where have you been?" Chief asked.

"Bruna and I went for a run."

"Well, next time tell someone before you take off. I almost called the MPs." The MPs were the military police.

"Wash up," Mom said. "Dinner is going to get cold."

A few minutes later, I joined my family. Across the table, Sam was still frowning at me.

That kid was talented. She could pout and chew at the same time. Only I didn't frown back. I smiled because now I knew what to draw. As I chewed my meatloaf, each picture formed in my mind.

After dinner, I popped out of my chair, thankful it was Tori's turn to do the dishes. That meant I could start the illustrations for *Princess Samantha, Ruler of the Fair Land of NAS Pensacola.*

Before I dashed off, though, Chief asked, "Piper, don't you have any homework?"

The words *Cyrus McCormick* flashed in my head. But that report wasn't due until next week. I had plenty of time. "I don't have any homework due tomorrow."

Chief studied me a long moment before saying, "In that case, at ease."

"Yes sir." I saluted him before taking off for my bedroom.

Since Sam did her homework at the kitchen table, I could draw in privacy. It's hard to believe a first-grader had so many assignments. But Sam liked homework.

I drew until it was time for lights out. Then I hid the drawing pad and flashlight under my pillow just as Sam came into the room and changed into her pajamas. When I heard Sam's

heavy breathing, I pulled out the pad and turned
on the flashlight. I drew until I fell asleep with
my face in the sketch pad.

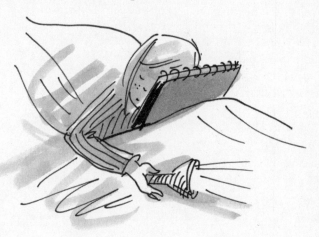

The next morning, I awoke to Sam's squeal. My eyes popped wide open. The first thing I saw was Sam, holding my drawings. "I love them!" she said. "I love the pictures!"

8

COUNTDOWN

I was happy Sam liked the illustrations. Before my walk yesterday, I had trouble thinking of any pictures because I knew a princess couldn't really rule a military base. But when I let myself pretend, everything became possible. I sang the entire way to school and hummed down the school hall on the way to class. Then Ms. Gordon announced, "It's time to turn in the first draft of your biographical paper."

"What?" I asked Michael, who was snapping

open his three-ring binder. He pulled out some pages.

"The biographical paper," Michael whispered. "You know, the one you're doing on that guy who invented pepper."

"Cyrus McCormick didn't invent pepper. He invented the reaper."

Ms. Gordon stared my way. "Piper, where's your first draft?"

I shrugged. "I think I must have been absent the day you assigned that."

Ms. Gordon sighed. "Piper Reed, you haven't missed one day of school since you transferred here last year. Believe me, I'd remember."

"Well, maybe I was in the bathroom or in Mrs. Mitchell's room."

Ms. Gordon's eyelid began to twitch. "Piper, you were given a list when I assigned the paper that clearly stated the due dates."

Kami held out her list to Ms. Gordon.

"Thank you, Kami." Ms. Gordon showed me Kami's list. "This is it."

"May I see that?"

Ms. Gordon handed the paper to me.

Sure enough, it looked kind of familiar, but I'd never gotten around to reading the first sentence. Keeping up with all this school stuff was hard when I was running a business. Not to mention, I was now an illustrator and a substitute babysitter, too.

Ms. Gordon collected the papers, then told us to turn to page 37 in our math notebooks.

I dug out the notebook and started to work on the first problem. I hated word problems. The letters wouldn't stay still and I had to read them ten times before I understood.

Before I could read this one a second time, Ms. Gordon said, "Piper, please come here a moment."

I swallowed. This didn't sound good.

"May I see your note cards?" she asked.

"Note cards?" Ms. Gordon was filled with all sorts of surprise questions today.

"The index cards with notes from your

research. That was step one. The cards were to help you write step two—your first draft."

"Well, um . . ."

"Just as I suspected. You haven't started on your report yet, have you, Piper? Do you even know who Cyrus McCormick is?"

"Sure. Cyrus McCormick was the inventor of the reaper."

"And?" Her face froze, except for that twitching eyelid.

"And . . . he really was."

"Really was what?"

"The inventor of the reaper."

Ms. Gordon wrote a hall pass, then handed it to me. "Piper, take your notebook and go to the library. Start your research on Cyrus McCormick." She talked in a soft voice, but that didn't stop the class from staring our way. When someone whispers, it makes people want to eavesdrop.

"But I thought it was math time."

"I guess you'll have more homework tonight. Your report is due Monday morning. This is a very important assignment. If you keep neglecting projects throughout the year, you'll end up repeating fifth grade."

My stomach sank on the way back to my desk. I pictured myself sitting in the same class-room with other kids, kids I didn't know. Michael wasn't there. Hailey and Nicole weren't there either.

Before leaving for the library, I went up to Ms. Gordon and asked, "Ms. Gordon, are you going to be teaching fifth grade again next year?"

Ms. Gordon didn't answer. She just took a big breath and pointed at the door.

In the library, Mrs. Keller met me with a smile. I liked fluffy Mrs. Keller. She reminded me of someone who wanted to sing "Jingle Bells" all year long.

"Piper, I'm surprised I didn't see you last week. Did you just now get my note?"

"What note?"

"The note that I slipped into your student mailbox."

"Oh, that mailbox. I never check that."

"Piper, maybe you should. My note would have told you I'd ordered a couple of books about Cyrus McCormick for the library. I figured some other student would probably be assigned a report on him in the future."

Yeah, I thought, some other poor student.

"Would you like to check them out?"

"I guess so." My homework was piling up by the minute. "Are there any pictures in those books?"

Mrs. Keller scanned them. "Yes, this one has more than the other. But the other book has a lot of interesting facts. Did you know that Cyrus McCormick's father worked on a horse-drawn reaper for years?"

By the time I got home I was exhausted. I didn't know where to start. Finish Sam's illustrations? Or start on the Cyrus McCormick research? I'd about decided to finish Sam's illustrations when the phone rang. Hailey didn't even say hello. She just yelled, "Where's that rabbit?"

Mr. Sanchez said we could borrow his rabbit the day before the party. He said he couldn't let us have the rabbit earlier because he owned only one and somebody might buy it. "I hope you understand, Piper, but it's a business decision."

"Well, maybe *I* could buy the rabbit." It could be a business expense. "How much is it, Mr. Sanchez?"

"Fifty-seven dollars."

I gulped. Being in business could be expensive. "I guess we'll wait for Friday." Until then, Hailey would just have to practice with Mr. Bunny.

Thursday night I finished the last illustration for Sam's book. The school secretary said we could make copies on their color printer if we used our own paper. Sam bought the paper with some of the savings from her piggy bank.

Friday after school, Mom, Sam, and I became a publishing company. Mom used the school copier while Sam stacked the pages and I stapled. We made one hundred copies. The book was twenty-five pages long. Ten of those pages were my pictures.

The cover showed Princess Samantha looking over the base from the lighthouse. Bold letters spelled out **PRINCESS SAMANTHA, RULER**

OF THE FAIR LAND OF NAS PENSACOLA BY SAMANTHA REED. Underneath in tiny letters— ILLUSTRATIONS BY PIPER REED. I was lucky to even have my name on the book. Mom made her include me. She told her, "Sam, that book wouldn't be the same without your sister's art."

And later Mom said to me, "Piper, you're really good. Maybe you'll be an illustrator when you grow up."

Mom's compliment made me feel like hollering "Get off the bus!" but I reminded her, "I'm going to be a Blue Angel."

By the time we finished, it was 5:30. So Mom called Chief and asked him to meet us at White Sands Seafood Grill for dinner.

When we arrived, Tori and Chief were already there. Chief was flipping through his *Outdoorsman* catalog, staring at the tents. Ever since he came home from his last ship duty, he'd talked about taking us camping. The only thing

Tori would stop studying words for was food. Nothing could get between her and French fries, not even five thousand dollars.

I wondered how she thought she'd win anyway. She'd wasted days memorizing those itty-bitty words when she should have studied long words like Sam used in her book.

That night I could hear Tori making her list of tiny words through the vent. I thought about tomorrow and everything I had to do—babysit the triplets, decorate for Brady's party and make sure it was a great success. A million butterflies zoomed around in my belly. Maybe they didn't have anything to do with all the things I had planned for the next day. Maybe I was hungry.

I went to the kitchen for a peanut butter cookie. Sam sat at the table with a stack of her books. She wore her crown and a pink princess costume she'd chosen for Halloween. Mom and

Chief had bought a pink feather pen for her book signing. She held it a few inches above one of the books and swept it through the air as if she was signing her name. A big grin spread across her face as she held the book out to no one and said, "You are welcome very much."

"What are you doing?" I asked her.

"I'm having a dress rehearsal."

"A book-signing dress rehearsal?" Both of my sisters were wasting their time. Tori, memorizing her tiny words, was sure to lose. And Sam, rehearsing her book signing, would be lucky if she sold one copy. I grabbed a cookie and went upstairs to bed.

9

Saturday

Saturday morning everyone buzzed around in a hurry. We were all getting ready to go to different places. Chief was going with Tori to the Scrabble championship, Mom was taking Sam to the book signing, and I was heading to my first job of the day.

As usual, Mom misplaced her car keys and hunted around for them.

Even Sam was looking for them because she was afraid she'd be late. She tiptoed around the room holding the skirt of her pink costume as she poked her head in closets.

When Mom found the keys between the couch cushions, she headed toward the door, then froze.

Mom swung around, facing us. "I've been meaning to ask you, Tori, who did you get to fill in for babysitting today?"

Tori's face turned red. She didn't say a word.

"Me!" I shouted.

"Piper?" Mom and Chief hollered at the same time.

"Mom! Come on!" Sam said.

Mom walked over to Tori. "Piper has never babysat except to stay with Sam an hour or so at a time."

"I'm not a baby," Sam said. "I'm an author."

Mom plopped down onto the couch.

"I can do it," I said. "Piper Reed Substitute Babysitting Service is responsible."

Then the strangest thing happened. Tori said, "Piper is one of the most responsible people I know."

Chief narrowed his eyes and smirked.

Sam bounced in place, causing her crown to slide to the right a bit. "Mom! We're going to be late for a very important date."

Tori joined in, "I'm going to be late, too, Dad."

"You have us at a disadvantage, girls," Chief said. "This should have been discussed with us before now."

"Does Mrs. Milton know?" Mom asked.

"Yes," said Tori. "Now can we go? I'm going to be back by one o'clock anyway."

A bunch of lines appeared on Mom's forehead. "Well, it is just for a few hours."

"Tell you what," Chief said, digging in his pocket. "Take my cell phone, Piper. Call your mom if something comes up that you can't deal with. Okay?"

"Yes sir," I said with a salute.

Mom and Sam left for Mr. Sanchez's. And Chief dropped me off at the Miltons' before heading with Tori to the Scrabble championship. I took my sack of supplies for Brady's party.

As Chief pulled up in front of the Miltons'

house, Tori said, "Just a word of warning—*don't* give them sugar."

"Who would do something dumb like that?" I asked. As if I'd let six-year-olds near a sugar bowl.

Mrs. Milton opened the door. She wore a lime green suit, matching shoes, and a beaded fuchsia necklace. Her bright red hair flipped up at the shoulders. She stared at me, starting at my head and ending at my toes. Then she did it again. Maybe I should have worn something a little fancier. She was a decorator after all.

Finally she said, "Can I help you?"

"I'm Piper Reed, the babysitter substitute service."

"Tori's sister? Just how old are you?"

"I'm almost eleven." I sounded like Brady. I'd just turned ten a couple of months ago.

"Oh. Well, I guess that's old enough." Then her mood switched and she started talking fast.

"You don't know how grateful I am to see you. This is the biggest decorating job I've ever had, and today I have to meet the drapery installers. We're installing drapes in eight rooms. I might be a little late."

"No problem," I said. I didn't have to worry. Tori would return from the competition at one o'clock, and I'd be able to leave for Brady's.

"Have you met the boys?" Mrs. Milton asked.

"I've seen them at school." They were first-graders. One was in Sam's class.

Mrs. Milton winked. "Don't mention it to him, but I think Timmy has a little crush on your sister Samantha."

I followed Mrs. Martin down the hall as her high heels clicked against the tiled floor. In the living room, two ladder-back chairs held up a blanket, forming a tent.

"Boys!" she hollered.

Three redheaded boys popped out from under the tent. They looked exactly alike except each wore a different color T-shirt.

Mrs. Milton pointed to each boy as she named them. "That's Tommy in red, Timmy in blue, and Todd in brown. Boys, this is Piper Reed, Tori's sister."

All three stared at the floor and peered up at me, smiling shyly. "Hi," they mumbled.

Mrs. Milton grabbed her purse. "Now you

need to treat Piper with the same respect you give Tori. Understand?"

They nodded. "Yes, ma'am."

Babysitting the triplets was going to be a breeze.

"Help yourself to anything you want to eat, Piper. The boys know where everything is. And if you don't mind, please make ham sandwiches for them around noon." She swung a giant tote bag over her shoulder and waved like a beauty queen as she headed toward the door. "Have a good day."

I tried counting in my head all the money I was going to make today from babysitting, Brady's party, and Sam's book sales. I doubted there'd be much from the book sales though. How many people would buy a princess book when they really wanted a new puppy? But with a little luck, a few people might feel sorry for Sam.

Just as I was estimating the total amount, the boys hollered, "Charge!"

A second later, I lay flat on my stomach. One triplet sat on my back, a second straddled my legs. The third held my arm down. I was the victim of a triple tackle.

"Get off me!" I squirmed, trying to wriggle free.

Tori was right. I needed that football helmet. The harder I tried to get up, the harder they pushed back. Finally I decided to give them the Piper Reed Last-Chance-Maneuver. I played dead.

"Is she faking?" asked Timmy or Tommy or Todd.

"Of course she is."

"Pinch her."

A triplet pinched my arm so hard I felt tears form behind my eyelids. But I stayed quiet.

Finally, one by one, they got bored and left me alone. Then Tommy turned on the television. Cartoons blared. I stood and tiptoed out of the living room, looking for a clock. The clock radio in Mrs. Milton's bedroom read 9:25. Great. Tori wouldn't return for hours. This was the worst job ever. No wonder she wanted to quit.

My muscles throbbed. Red welts formed on my arm. I couldn't wait to leave. At least for now they were hypnotized under the spell of cartoons. I joined them at a safe distance, selecting a chair at the back of the room.

At noon, I made ham sandwiches. I cut off

the crusts since I figured most kids didn't like them. I bet Tori didn't do that. Then I poured potato chips into a huge bowl. I grabbed the blanket that they'd used for a tent and spread it outside on the grass.

While I smoothed out the wrinkles, the sliding glass door opened and a redhead popped out like a turtle peeking from its shell.

"Hey, what are you doing out there?" asked Tommy.

"We're going to have a picnic," I said, proud that I'd thought of something fun. I'm sure Tori never thought of any fun ideas like this. Why eat lunch inside the house when we could eat outside? The sky had turned gray, but a few clouds didn't have to spoil my plan.

Now all three boys stared my way.

"Grab the sandwiches and potato chips," I told them.

Instead, the door shut, followed by a *click!*

I tried to open the door. Locked.

I knocked. I got three waves. Score: Two for the Milton Monsters. Zero for Piper Reed. Then I noticed Chief's cell phone was on the kitchen table. Make that three for the Miltons.

The boys turned around and started to eat their sandwiches. A moment later they were throwing potato chips at one another. Then they lifted the cookie jar lid and dipped their hands inside. The more cookies they ate, the more rowdy they became, jumping from the kitchen chairs to the top of the table.

The sun peeked between the clouds. My face and neck burned. I flopped onto a lawn chair and waited for Tori. She'd be back soon.

About twenty minutes later Todd opened the door and handed the phone to me.

"It's for you. It's your ugly sister."

Just as I grabbed the cell phone and snapped,

"Don't call my sister ug—" he closed the door
and locked it again.

"Hello?"

Tori spoke quickly between short breaths.
"Piper, I hate to do this to you, but I need you to

stay at the Miltons' longer. I'm in the finals, and they're running late."

"I can't, Tori! Brady's party starts at three o'clock, and I have to be there early to decorate."

"The competition won't take long. Please, Piper! I have a good feeling about this."

I sized up the situation. Tori might win a lot of money while I was stuck with the Milton Monsters. She needed me to save the day. That should be worth something. Half of five thousand dollars would easily cover the costs of the clubhouse.

"Will you split the money with me?" I asked.

"Split the money?" she squealed. "No way."

"Sorry. I don't think I can help you. You'd better come back."

"Okay, okay. If I win first place, you can have half the money."

"Get off the bus!" I yelled, then hung up the phone.

I knocked on the sliding glass door.

Todd cracked open the door. "What's the magic password?" the boys asked together.

"How would you like to go to a birthday party?"

The door slid wide open.

Score one for Piper Reed.

10

PARTY TIME

Now I knew what Tori meant when she said keep the Milton triplets away from sugar. She meant *anything* with sugar. They'd finished off the entire contents of the cookie jar. Now they were bouncing around like Ping-Pong balls.

"You have to hold hands," I told them as we took off for Brady's house. It was just a few streets away from the Miltons' home, but there was no telling what those three would do. They might run down the middle of the street or race in a different direction.

Each triplet carried a wrapped gift. They'd insisted on bringing gifts for Brady, so they'd all picked out their least favorite toy.

Timmy picked a bear with a missing arm. Tommy chose a computer game that he was tired of. Todd wanted to give him all his books because he hated to read. But I made him pick one. We even found some cool striped wrapping paper in the hall closet. It was kind of stiff and hard to fold. Tape wouldn't hold it down, but I found a big container of paste in the same closet and it worked great.

I didn't have a key, so I locked the front door from the inside before shutting it. That's when I thought about leaving a note. Oh well, Tori would return home soon and see that we were at Brady's. I hope she won first place because I couldn't wait to buy the club-house.

The boys sang as we walked down the street—"We're going to a party, a birthday party, some boy named Brady's birthday party. We're going to a party."

Soon we arrived and Brady answered the door.

"Happy birthday, Brady. Look, I brought you more guests and gifts."

"Oh boy!" Then he counted them. "One, two, twee. I want to be twee, too."

"You are three," I told him.

"No. I want to be twee boys like them." He pointed to the Miltons.

"They're triplets," I said.

"Yeah," Timmy said. "We have the same birthday. I'm the oldest."

"By one minute," Todd said.

Timmy corrected him. "One minute and seventeen seconds."

"Can we come inside?" I asked. "I need to help your mom decorate for your party."

"Birthday party!" the Milton triplets sang out the song they'd made up. "Someone named Brady's birthday party."

"That's me!" He swung the door wide open.

Yolanda was spreading a tablecloth on the kitchen table. She looked up and her jaw dropped when she saw the Milton triplets.

"I hope you don't mind," I said. "I had to invite them because Tori is in the Scrabble championship finals and I'm babysitting them for her."

Tommy was taking a spin around the house. When he whizzed by us, Yolanda waved her arm toward him, but he'd already disappeared. Her mouth opened, but words didn't come out. Finally she managed, "Scrabble? Triplets?"

"Tori babysits the Milton triplets every Saturday, but she's competing in a Scrabble championship. I told her I'd babysit. She was supposed to finish at one, but the finals are running late. That's why I had to bring the boys. I wanted to get here on time."

Yolanda didn't say anything.

"Don't worry. They brought gifts."

Now all three Miltons were dashing around the house, but this time Brady tagged behind, calling out, "Wait for me!"

"Boys!" Yolanda yelled.

The boys froze. So did I. I'd never heard Yolanda scream before.

Then her voice turned soft again. "Boys, if you want to play inside the house you cannot run. I have a better idea: Why don't you play in the backyard?"

Yolanda and I followed them outside. We hung paper planets and stars over the porch and covered the picnic table with a shiny silver paper cloth. Then we placed the gifts on the table.

The boys played on the swing set. This was the best they'd been all day. Maybe I should have tried that scary scream like Yolanda used.

Next I opened the
sack and pulled out
the Martian antennas.

Yolanda smiled when I
modeled a pair. "Piper, did
you make those?"

I nodded. They'd
taken me two after-
noons. I'd worked on
them right after school
and didn't stop until
bedtime.

Yolanda fixed a pair

on top of her head and spoke in an alien voice. "You-are-so-cre-a-tive."

"Thank-you-very-much," I said in the same funny tone.

By the time we'd finished hanging the stars and planets, Nicole and Michael arrived.

Nicole wore striped pajamas and a green wig. A gigantic pair of blue flippers covered her feet.

"What's with the flippers?" I asked. "Are you going swimming?"

"Clowns are supposed to have big feet. I tried to wear my dad's sneakers, but they kept slipping off. Guess what though! I can juggle!"

Her braces looked shiny through the big red grin painted across her white clown makeup. "I practiced and practiced. Practice makes perfect," Nicole said.

Michael carefully set a box on the table. He

undid the box at the corners and slid the chocolate triple-decker cake out. It looked delicious!

I dug through my decorations and pulled out

the three astronauts and the spaceship for the cake.

When I started to position them on the cake, Michael grabbed my wrist. "Hey, if you think you're going to do the finishing touches after I baked every day for the last couple of weeks, you must be from Mars."

"Go ahead," I said, even though *I'd* made the finishing touches.

Finally Hailey arrived. She rode up on her bicycle, wearing a black cape and a top hat. The rabbit sat in a cage inside her handlebar basket. She came to a quick stop. Then she grabbed the cage before letting the bike fall to the ground.

Marching toward us, Hailey held the cage away from her body as if the rabbit had some contagious disease. "I hate this rabbit! I hate it! I hate it! Ever since my dad picked it up last night from Mr. Sanchez's, it's been scratching and nibbling me. It thinks I'm a carrot!"

I pressed my finger against my lips. "Shhhh! You're going to ruin the surprise."

"I don't care!" she yelled. "I wish I'd never said I'd do this. I wish I'd picked baking the cake, or, better yet, I should have never agreed to be a part of your birthday party planning business. *We* did all the work while *you* got to be in charge."

I rushed away from her, not because it was all I could think to do but because Brady was in triplet trouble. He clung to the crossbar of the swing set while the boys shook it hard.

Brady didn't seem to mind though. He just yelled, "Faster, faster, faster!"

"Stop!" I yelled, rushing toward the boys.

But the triplets shook the swing set harder until it tottered like a seesaw. The legs came out of the ground, leaving holes.

Then one of Brady's hands lost its grip on the bar and the tone of his voice changed. "Stop, stop, stop!"

Yolanda raced over, her antennas bouncing. She screamed, "Quit that right this very minute!"

I froze.

The triplets released their grasp on the swing set and Brady fell, landing like a pretzel on the ground.

"My arm hurts," he cried. "It hurts bad."

When Yolanda gently touched his arm, Brady shouted.

Yolanda's forehead wrinkled. "I hope his arm isn't broken. I'd better take him to the clinic to check it out."

Just as they drove off, Tori and Mrs. Milton were taking wide strides across the yard. Mrs. Milton's high heels made holes in the grass, but she didn't seem to care. "Come on, boys. We're leaving this minute."

"But we're at a birthday party," said Timmy.

"Someone named Brady's birthday party," added Todd.

"He's my best friend," said Tommy.

At that moment, Mrs. Milton noticed the table with the gifts. A long gasp flew from her mouth. She swung around, facing me. "Is that my client's wallpaper? You used it as wrapping paper?"

I didn't have time to explain. Mrs. Milton grabbed the gifts and ordered the triplets to follow her.

Sam showed up with a gift for Brady, but Mrs. Milton stomped straight past her. When

Timmy saw Sam, he froze and stared at her with a dumb look on his face. "Hi, Samantha!"

Sam straightened her tiara. "I'm an author. I sold a hundred books at my signing."

"Wow," Timmy said.

"Timmy!" yelled Mrs. Milton.

"Bye, Samantha." Timmy ran to meet his mom at the car.

Once they'd climbed into their car, I asked Tori, "Did you win?"

She didn't answer. Instead her face turned red and her eyes bulged like a steam cap on a teakettle. "Piper Reed, you're in trouble!"

11

~~~

Due Date

The only person who looked happy about Brady's party ending before it even started was Hailey. I'll bet she never learned to pull that rabbit out of a hat.

Mrs. Milton told Tori she could babysit next week. But she had to promise to never get a substitute, especially if that substitute was named Piper Reed.

While Abe and Yolanda were at the clinic with Brady, Chief secured Brady's swing set to the ground with ropes. "There," he said when he finished. "That should be triplet safe."

Then he wiped his hands on a rag and turned to me. "Piper, we need to have a long talk."

If I'd made a list from Chief's talk, this is what would be on it:

1. Babysitting is a job for a responsible person.
2. I have not proven to be responsible.
3. Leave a note when I take someone's kids somewhere.
4. Do not invite people to a party unless it is my party.
5. It's better to do one job well than three jobs poorly.

Even though a lot of things went wrong that day, some things went right. Brady didn't break his arm, though he did have a bad sprain. Tori didn't win the competition, but she did win third place—five hundred dollars—which was not enough money to go on the trip to England but was a lot more than she could earn babysitting

the Milton triplets for an entire summer. Unfortunately she didn't split that money with me because she said she only agreed to split the money if she won first place. It's the tiny details that always do you in. When I asked her how she won third place, she said, "Little words with big point values."

Probably the biggest surprise of the whole day was that Sam sold all hundred copies of her book. At one dollar each, that was fifty dollars for her and fifty for me.

"It was amazing," Mom said. "People came into the store and they'd leave with a pet and two books. Almost everyone bought more than one."

That evening, the phone rang. After Mom hung up, she said, "We have forgiving neighbors. Yolanda and Abe have invited us over to celebrate Brady's birthday tonight."

Brady's little playmates were there. Michael, Nicole, and Hailey came, too. There was no sign of a rabbit, but Hailey and Nicole wore their costumes. Later we ate Michael's cake while Nicole entertained us by juggling. Then Hailey performed three card tricks.

The birthday party was spectacular until Hailey asked, "Did you finish your biographical paper, Piper?"

She was still trying to get back at me because of that rabbit. Mom and Chief looked at me, waiting.

"Not quite," I said.

My parents didn't say anything until we got
home.

"Two things, Piper," Chief said. Even when

he wasn't making lists he spoke like he was writing one. He continued, "Abe and Yolanda wanted to pay you a hundred dollars for the party planning."

"A hundred dollars? Is it a hundred-dollar bill?" I'd never seen a hundred-dollar bill.

"Yes, but I told them absolutely not. You should be paying *them* after the big mess you caused."

"Oh," I mumbled. I guess I still wasn't going to see what a hundred-dollar bill looked like.

"Second, you haven't finished writing your paper, which is due this Monday. How much have you done so far?"

"I have the research books," I told him.

Chief sighed. "That's a start. Guess what job you have tomorrow?"

I swallowed. "Cyrus McCormick?"

"Affirmative," said Chief.

Cyrus McCormick. I decided to start by writing everything I knew about him. Cyrus McCormick was a man. Cyrus McCormick invented the reaper. It doesn't take long to write everything you know about your subject when it amounts to two sentences. I opened one of the books and looked at all the pictures. Then I began to read.

I learned that Cyrus McCormick always liked to invent things, even when he was fifteen years old. And like Mrs. Keller said, his dad had worked on a horse-drawn reaper for years, but it was Cyrus who'd invented the final version. And even then, he had help from Jo Anderson, his assistant.

It made me think about Sam's book. My pictures were great, but I couldn't have drawn them without Sam's story.

And Brady ended up having a super birthday

party, but it wasn't just because of me. I couldn't have done it without the other Gypsy Club members. And even if she'd never admit it, Tori couldn't have won third place in that Scrabble championship if I hadn't babysat the Milton triplets.

The next day when I handed my report in with my classmates', Ms. Gordon seemed surprised. "Piper, did you learn anything that you

would do different the next time you're assigned a project like this?"

"Yes, ma'am, I sure did. *Next time* I'll make sure I hurry and write my name next to Amelia Earhart's before Kami does."

Ms. Gordon really ought to see a doctor about that twitching eye.

At recess, Michael said, "I guess we're never going to have that clubhouse, are we? Those triplets ruined everything."

When he said that, it made me think about when I first met the triplets.

"Does a clubhouse have to be a house?" I asked.

Hailey scowled. "What do you mean does it have to be a house? It's called a club*house*, isn't it?"

"I have an idea," I told them. "Meet me at my home after school."

Hailey smirked. "Piper, why do we always have to meet at your home whenever you have a 'great' idea?"

Then I told her, "When you have a great idea, we'll meet at your home."

Later at the meeting I showed the Gypsy Club page 94 of Chief's *Outdoorsman* catalog. "Look." I pointed to the tent.

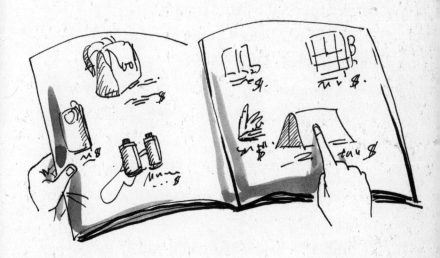

"It's rainproof," Michael read aloud.

"And pest proof," I added. The zipper opening could be closed from the inside to keep out pests like Sam.

"Only one problem," Hailey said. "It costs forty-nine ninety-nine."

"No problem," I said. "I have fifty dollars." Thanks to my illustrations in Sam's book.

"Get off the bus!" we yelled, doing a happy dance around the living room.

Suddenly Michael stopped dancing. "Wait a minute. What about the tax?"

It's always the little details that can do you in.

"I have an idea," Nicole said. "Let's have a bake sale!"

"That's a good idea," Michael said. "Our freezer has enough cupcakes to cover a lot of tax."

"Super," I said. "We could call it the Gypsy

Club Chocolate Cupcakes for Tax Sale. All in favor?"

Michael, Nicole, and I shouted "Aye!" but Hailey was silent.

She fixed her hands on her hips. "Why do you have to name everything, Piper Reed?"

I told her, "When you think of a great name, we'll use it. By the way, did you ever learn to pull a rabbit out of a hat?"

For the first time ever, Hailey didn't snap back. She stayed quiet a moment, then said, "Okay. I like the name."

"All in favor of the Gypsy Club Chocolate Cupcakes for Tax Sale?"

This time, we all said "Aye!"

The Gypsy Club was on the job again.

KIMBERLY WILLIS HOLT

What did you want to be when you grew up?
A writer.

When did you realize you wanted to be a writer?
In seventh grade, three teachers encouraged my writing. That was when I first thought the dream could come true. Before that, I didn't think I could be a writer because I wasn't a great student and I read slowly.

What's your first childhood memory?
Buying an orange Dreamsicle from the ice-cream man. I was two years old.

What's your most embarrassing childhood memory?
In fourth grade, I tried to impress the popular girls that I wanted to be friends with by doing somersaults in front of them. (I never learned to do cartwheels.) They called me a showoff, so I guess it didn't work. If only I'd known how to do a cartwheel.

What was your worst subject in school?
Algebra.

What was your first job?
I was in the movies. I popped popcorn at the Westside Cinemas.

How did you celebrate publishing your first book?
I'm sure my family went out to dinner. We always celebrate by eating.

Where do you write your books?
I write several places—a soft, big chair in my bedroom, at a table on my screen porch, or at coffee shops.

Where do you find inspiration for your writing?
Most of the inspiration for my writing comes from moments in my childhood.

Which of your characters is most like you?
I'm a bit like most of them. However, I fashioned Tori in the Piper Reed books after me. But Tori is bossier than I was and she certainly makes better grades than I did.

When you finish a book, who reads it first?
My daughter listens to me read my first draft.

Are you a morning person or a night owl?
I'm a morning person.

 SQUARE FISH

What's your idea of the best meal ever?
That's a toss-up. My grandmother's chicken and dumplings, and sushi.

Which do you like better: cats or dogs?
I'm a dog person. I have a poodle named Bronte who is the model for Bruna.

What do you value most in your friends?
Loyalty and honesty.

Where do you go for peace and quiet?
Home.

Who is your favorite fictional character?
Leroy in *Mister and Me* because he is forgiving. And that's a trait many of us don't have.

What are you most afraid of?
Anything harming my daughter.

What time of the year do you like best?
Fall.

What is your favorite TV show?
CBS Sunday Morning.

If you were stranded on a desert island, who would you want for company?
My husband and daughter.

What's the best advice you have ever received about writing?
A writer once told me, "Readers either see what they read or hear what they read. Writers have to learn to write for both." When I started following that advice, my writing improved.

What do you want readers to remember about your books?
The characters. I want them to seem like real people. I want them to miss them and wonder what happened to them.

What would you do if you ever stopped writing?
I plan on dying with a pen in my hand.

What do you like best about yourself?
I'm honest.

What is your worst habit?
I eat too much.

What do you consider to be your greatest accomplishment?
I gave birth to a wonderful human being.

What do you wish you could do better?
I wish I could do a cartwheel.

What would your readers be most surprised to learn about you?
I send gift cards with positive messages to myself when I order something for me.

*K*eep reading for an excerpt from
Piper Reed: Into the Wild,
available in hardcover from Henry Holt.

EXCERPT

Halloween was two weeks away. Trick-or-treating and jack-o'-lanterns—that was all I could think about. But I still hadn't decided on my costume. I thought about dressing as a Blue Angel pilot for the U.S. Navy since that's what I planned to be when I grew up. But I didn't own a Blue Angel's uniform.

On the way to school, I asked, "Do you think the base is going to do anything special for Halloween?" We lived at NAS Pensacola because our dad was a Navy chief.

"I'm going to be someone that I've never been before," my little sister, Sam, said.

"Who?"

"Princess Elizabeth."

"What's new about that?" I asked. "You're a princess every year." Sam would use any excuse to wear her crown.

Sam frowned. "I've never been Princess Elizabeth before."

"I thought she was *Queen* Elizabeth." I knew some things about the royal family.

"Queens have to be princesses first," said Sam.

"What are you going to be?" I asked Tori.

My big sister was sitting in the front seat with Mom. We had to drop her off at the middle school before Mom drove us to the elementary school where we went and where she worked as the art teacher.

Tori didn't answer me so I spoke louder. "Well, what are you going to be?"

She turned around and rolled her eyes. "Piper, Halloween is for little kids. I'm almost thirteen. I don't do dress up."

"You mean you have to stop having fun when you're a teenager?" I was sure glad I was in fifth grade. That meant I still had a few good years left.

"I'll stay home and give out the candy," Tori said.

"Gosh," I said, "the trick-or-treaters won't stand a chance." My sister loved to eat. She'd probably empty the candy bowl before the first goblin rang our doorbell.

Tori glared at me. "Piper Reed, you're mean." Then her head snapped in Mom's direction. "Mom!"

Mom wasn't a morning person. She needed coffee. Lots of coffee. She probably didn't hear one word I said, but she went into her warning tone. "Girls, behave. It's too early for this."

Before the bell rang I met the other Gypsy Club members. We gathered in our usual spot near the front of the school sign. The twins, Michael and Nicole, were already there. But this time there was someone else standing in our circle—a boy with hair that stuck straight up like he forgot to comb it.

Hailey hopped off the bus and raced across the school yard. When she caught up with me, she asked, "Who's that boy?"

"I don't know, but he's in our meeting place."

"Hi, Piper." Nicole flashed her braces. She must have gone to the orthodontist because yesterday her rubber bands were fuchsia. Today she wore orange and black ones.

"Hi," I said, but I was staring at the new kid. He had the thickest glasses I'd ever seen on anyone.

"This is Stanley Hampshire," Michael said. "He just moved here." He punched Stanley's shoulder. He acted like Stanley was his new best friend.

"Oh," I said. "Hi, Stanley. I'm sorry, but this is a Gypsy Club meeting spot."

Hailey snapped, "Piper, you're mean!"

That was the second time I'd heard that today and the morning bell hadn't even rang yet. Hailey was right. I was being mean. My dad was a Navy chief. I knew what it was like being the new kid. I'd moved a zillion times.

"I . . . I was thinking," Michael stammered. "I was thinking Stanley could be in our Gypsy Club."

I gave Stanley a good look over. I'd only lived here in Pensacola a year. That first day was hard until I started the Gypsy Club.

"He meets all the qualifications," Michael said. "His dad is in the Navy. He moves a lot, too. And he already knows the Gypsy Club creed."

"What?" I yelled.

Everyone stared at me.

"You taught him the Gypsy Club creed without asking permission of your fellow Gypsy Club members?"

Michael folded his arms across his chest. "I don't remember that being a rule."

"Well, some rules shouldn't have to be spoken."

"Am I supposed to read your mind?"

Stanley stared down at the ground. He was probably real smart and read lots of books. Smart people had to wear glasses because they wore out their eyes from reading all those books. That meant my eyes had a lifetime guarantee.

Nicole spoke up. "I don't see anything wrong with Stanley being in the Gypsy Club. It's hard to be new and make friends."

Without saying a word, Stanley glanced around the playground. I guess he was the silent type. The smart, silent type, who had replaced me as Michael's best friend.

Everyone scowled at me. My face burned. I knew when I was outnumbered. Sometimes even a captain has to listen to her soldiers. I saluted him. "Welcome to the Gypsy Club, Stanley!"

All of a sudden, Stanley opened his mouth real wide and shouted, "Get off the bus!"

Then he started to talk very fast. "I mean thanks. You're really not going to regret this. I've never been a member of a club before, but I think I'll be good at it. I once was in the Boy Scouts of America. That's not really a club. The Boy Scouts of America is an organization, but, anyway, I was only a member for a short while. I never earned a badge though. I wanted to earn the knot-tying badge. I really wanted that one bad because my dad is a sailor. I mean, he's an officer, but he sails for a hobby. I go with him sometimes, but I'm not very good at it. Now my brother Simon—"

The school bell rang. Kids raced by us and went inside the building. I usually dreaded that sound, but now I knew what it meant to be saved by the bell!

Nicole took off for her class while Hailey and I followed the boys. I wasn't sure about this new kid, Stanley. He'd already weaseled his way into the Gypsy Club. Now he was going to be in my class, too. That added up to a lot of Stanley Hampshire. At least he lived in the officer housing instead of the enlisted housing. That way I wouldn't be bumping into him on my street.

As usual Ms. Gordon made a big to do about Stanley being the new kid. She always made it sound like a new kid was a gift to our class. "Students," she said, "may I present Stanley Hampshire. He moved here from Norfolk, Virginia. Stanley, would you like to tell us a little about yourself?"

Uh-oh. For a teacher, Ms. Gordon sure had a lot to learn.

Stanley stood like he was running for mayor of Pensacola, Florida. He pushed up his glasses. He cleared his throat. "Well, my name is Stanley Hampshire, but you already know that. I was born in Germany, but I don't remember a thing about it because we moved by the time I was six months old, although my mom said I lived there long enough to develop a taste for Wiener schnitzel. But my dad says that's a fairy tale. Next we moved to Bremerton, Washington, and apparently we could see Mount Rainier from our backyard, but I don't remember that either because we moved before I was three. Then after that—"

Ms. Gordon said, "Okay, Stanley, thank you."

"But I didn't get to tell you about the other places I lived or what my favorite color is or my favorite television show."

Ms. Gordon's right eyelid started twitching. "That's quite all right, Stanley. We need to start our day."

Stanley looked disappointed. "Well, all right, if you say so." He sat down.

Right off, I could see that I was going to have to make a new rule for the Gypsy Club—Gypsy Club members must not be blabbermouths.

At lunch, Michael, Hailey, Nicole, and I learned everything the rest of the class missed.

Stanley had also lived in Groton, Connecticut, and in Hawaii. His favorite color was blue, not the blue of the sky but the blue on his fourth-grade geography textbook. He had two brothers and, according to Stanley, his oldest brother was the smartest human being in the world. "Simon will probably be president of the United States someday."

Stanley told us his favorite song was "Yankee Doodle." How could my favorite song be the same as his?

"'Yankee Doodle' makes me want to spin," said Stanley.

Hailey was about to take a bite when he said that. She put her sandwich down and asked, "Why?"

Stanley shrugged. "Beats me. I guess the rhythm makes me want to spin."

"'Yankee Doodle' makes me want to march," said Nicole.

"That's because 'Yankee Doodle' *is* a marching song," I said.

"If you say so," said Stanley. He chomped on his carrot and swallowed quickly. I knew what was coming next. More about Stanley Hampshire.

Right after lunch, Ms. Mitchell came into our classroom. I glanced at the clock. It was one thirty. I had already been to her room. She must miss me. Every morning I go to Ms. Mitchell's room. While the other kids have to read together in our classroom, I get to read alone with Ms. Mitchell. I have dyslexia.

I love Ms. Mitchell's room. It has an orange beanbag chair I sit in while I read. And she stashes stickers in her drawer—zillions of stickers. She lets me pick out a sticker for my notebook every time I read good . . . I mean, read well. That means I get a sticker every day because I've improved a lot since I started working with her last year. I grabbed my notebook and went to meet her at the front of the class.

"Hi, Piper," Ms. Mitchell said, smiling.

"Sit down, Piper," Ms. Gordon said.

"But I need to go to Ms. Mitchell's class," I told Ms. Gordon.

"Piper, I'm afraid it's not your turn," Ms. Mitchell said.

"But—"

Ms. Gordon's eye twitched. "Piper, please return to your seat." Then she said, "Stanley Hampshire, please come here and meet Ms. Mitchell."

Stanley stood and we passed each other on my return to my seat.

Ms. Gordon said, "Stanley Hampshire, this is your reading teacher, Ms. Mitchell."

Then Ms. Mitchell—*my* Ms. Mitchell—held out her hand. "Stanley, I can't wait to get to know you."

Uh-oh.

"Well," Stanley started, "I was born in Germany, which I don't remember a thing about because we moved when I was six months—"

"That's enough, Stanley," Ms. Gordon said. "You'll have plenty of time this year to tell Ms. Mitchell about yourself. For now it's time to read."

"But—"

"Go along now." Even from where I sat, I could see both of Ms. Gordon's eyes twitch.

JOIN IN THE FUN AND READ ALL THE
PIPER REED BOOKS
AVAILABLE FROM SQUARE FISH

A hilarious series about one spunky heroine with lots of spirit
trying to find her place in the world as the middle sister . . .

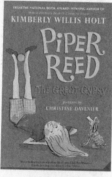

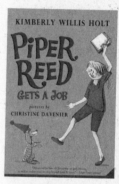

Kimberly Willis Holt Illustrated by Christine Davenier 978-0-312-38020-5 $6.99 US / $8.99 Can.	Kimberly Willis Holt Illustrated by Christine Davenier 978-0-312-56136-9 $6.99 US / $8.99 Can.	Kimberly Willis Holt Illustrated by Christine Davenier 978-0-312-60881-1 $6.99 US / $8.50 Can.

Meet Piper Reed, a spunky
nine-year-old who has moved
more times than she can count.
From Texas to Guam, wherever
Piper goes, adventure follows.

**"Piper's foray sets sail
with verve, fun and spunk."**
—*Kirkus Reviews*

Piper's dad might be gone again,
but she's got plenty to keep her
busy at home: new neighbors,
a spaceship beach house, a trip
to New Orleans, and most
important, the upcoming
Gypsy Club pet show!

Piper Reed and her fellow
Gypsy Club members are
in need of a clubhouse.
Raising money to buy one isn't
going to be easy. Fortunately for
Piper, her friends and family
come to her rescue!

**"A good addition to the
series . . . a natural for fans of
Clementine or Judy Moody."**
—*Kirkus Reviews*

Join the
Piper Reed
Club at
www.piperreed.com

SQUARE FISH

WWW.SQUAREFISHBOOKS.COM
AVAILABLE WHEREVER BOOKS ARE SOLD

ALSO AVAILABLE
FROM SQUARE FISH BOOKS

Five Stories to Laugh with and Love

Candyfloss · Jacqueline Wilson
Illustrated by Nick Sharratt
ISBN: 978-0-312-37132-6 · $5.99 US / $6.99 Can

*Move to a fabulous new home half-way
around the world with Mom,
or stay home with dear old Dad?*

★ "A poignant, gently humorous, and
totally satisfying tale. Flossie is
charmingly believable."
—*Booklist*, Starred Review

Everything on a Waffle · Polly Horvath
ISBN: 978-0-312-38004-5 · $6.99 US

*Haven't you ever just known something deep
in your heart without reason?*

★ "[A] tale of a (possibly) orphaned girl
from a small Canadian fishing village. . . .
A laugh-out-loud pleasure from
beginning to triumphant end."
—*Publishers Weekly*, Starred Review

Emmy and the Incredible Shrinking Rat
Lynne Jonell
Illustrated by Jonathan Bean
ISBN: 978-0-312-38460-9 · $6.99 US/$7.99 Can

*A lonely girl, a talking rat, and a nanny
whose doing VERY bad things!*

★ "A mystery is cleverly woven into this
fun and, at times, hilarious caper, and
children are likely to find themselves
laughing out loud."
—*School Library Journal*, Starred Review

The Giants and Joneses · Julia Donaldson
Illustrated by Greg Swearingen
ISBN: 978-0-312-37961-2 · $6.99 US

*The Joneses are about to be kidnapped
by giants!*

"An exciting story with a subtle
message about respect and cooperation."
—*School Library Journal*

Penina Levine Is a Hard-Boiled Egg · Rebecca O'Connell
Illustrated by Majella Lue Sue
ISBN: 978-0-312-55026-4 · $6.99 US/$7.99 Can

*Penina has a bossy best friend, a tattletale sister,
crazy parents, and a big, fat zero at school.*

"Penina is a feisty and thoroughly
enjoyable heroine with whom readers
will easily connect."
—*School Library Journal*

SQUARE FISH
WWW.SQUAREFISHBOOKS.COM
AVAILABLE WHEREVER BOOKS ARE SOLD